D1637330

A Fair Field

A retelling by:

Edward Brockert

(Οξφόρδη, Oriel της 79)

PAGE PUBLISHING, INC.
New York, NY

First originally published by Page Publishing, Inc. 2014

ISBN 978-1-62838-788-9 (pbk)
ISBN 978-1-62838-789-6 (digital)
ISBN 978-1-62838-790-2 (hardcover)

Printed in the United States of America

"I shall array me to ride

Rest thee a while"

—William Langland

1383

In a summer season,
  Whanne soft was the sun,
  I dressed in some shrouds
  As though I were a shepherd.

In this habit as an hermit,
Who would never work,
I went wide in this world
Wonders to hear.

But on a May morning,
On Malvern Hills,
There befell a marvel
Of fairy-me thought.

I was weary for wandering,
   And went me to rest
   Under a broad bank
   By a brook's side.

And as I lay and leaned
And looked in the waters,
I slumbered in a sleeping.
It swayed so merry.

Than began I to meter
This measure in the rhythm
Of a marvelous dream—
That I was in a wilderness.
I never knew where.

Triedlich Imaked

As I beheld in to the East,
On high to the sun,
I saw a tower on a toft,
So finely made.

A deep dale was beneath it,
A dungeon therein,
With deep ditches and dark
And dreadful of sight.

A fair field full of folk
Found I there between.
Of all manner of men,
The small and the rich,
Working and wandering
As the world asks.

Some put themselves to the plow.
        Playful seldom,
In setting their fields
        And sowing seeds,
They were working full hard.

All this I saw sleeping
And seven sights more.

I

What this mountain
Be'meaneth,
And the murky dale
And the field full of folk,
I shall now fair show.

A lovely alluring lady,
In linen y'clothed,
Came down from a castle
And called me fair,

And said, "Sleepiest thou?
See'st thou this people,
How busy they have been
About the maze?"

I was afraid of her face,
Though she fair were,
And said, "Mercy madam,
What is this
To mean?"

"The tower upon the toft,"
Quote she,
"Truth is there inne,
And would that you worked
 As his word teaches,
For truth is a treasure—
The choices on earth."

Then I friended her fairly,
  And asked,
"That dungeon in the dale,
That dreadful is of sight,
What may it be to mean madam?
I beseech you."

"That is the castle of care.
Whosoever comes there inne...?

I say, as I said before,
Whanne all treasures have been tried
Truth is the best.

Now have I told thee
What truth is.
That no treasure
Is better set in thine heart.
Thou shouldest been aware
I wisse thee the better."

"Madame mercy," quod I,
"I like your words well.
Ye must teach me better."

"I may no longer linger with thee.
Now you look,
Seek Sir Do~Well."

Thus I awaked, and wrote
What I had dreamed.

II

Thus, y'robed in <u>russet</u>,
      I roamed about
All a summer season,
      For to seek Sir Do~Well.

And friended full often,
Of folk that I meet,
To ask if any wit knew where
Do~Well was at Inne,

And what man he might be.
Of the many man I asked,
There was never wit,
As I went,
That could wisse me.

Until it befell on a Friday,
Two friars I meet,
    Masters of the Memories,
    Men of great wit.

I haylesade hem
heendeli as I hadde lerned

I called them friendlily,
As I had learned,
And prayed them
Their charity
Before they passed further,
If they knew of any country
Or coast as they had went,
"Where that Do~Well dwelleth,
Do me, to know."

For they have been
The men of this world
    That most while'd walk'en,
        And know of countries
            And courts
                And many kinds of places,
                Both princes' palaces
                And poor men's cottages
And do well and do evil,
Where they both dwell.

"Among us," quote the friars,
"That man is dwelling
And ever has,
As I hope,
And ever shall here~after."

"Contra," quote I, as a clerk,
And come-side to dispute
And said to them truly,
"He is not always
    Amongst you friars.
    He is other-while,
    Else-where,
        To wisse the people."

III

The king and his knights
    To the kirk went,
    To hear matins of the day
    And the mass after...

Thanne waked I of my winking,
And woe was with all
That I had not slept deeper,
And y'seen more.

But before I had gone,

Even a ways,

  A fantasy seized me,

   So that I might not

    Further a foot,

     For default of sleeping.

And I sat softly a dou'n,
And said my belief,
And so I babbled of my beads.
They brought me a sleep.

And thanne I saw much more
Then I before told,
   For I saw the field full of folk
      That I said of before...

IV

And thus I went wide,
Where, walking on my own,
 By a wild wilderness
            And by a wood side,
The bliss of the birds
            Brought me a sleep.

And under a tree,
Upon a land,
I leaned down a while
To join the lays
Those lovely fouls made.

The mervelououst
meteles mette I me than

The mirth of their mouths
Made me, there, to sleep.
The most marvelous melodies
Mette I,
me thanne,
That ever one dreamed
In the world~
As I suppose.

A man, as I thought,
And much like to myself,
Came and called me
By my proper name.

"What art thou," quoth I then,
  "That you know my name?"

"That thou were well," quod he,
  "And no manner better."

"Woot I," quote I, "what thou art?"

"Thought," said he then,
"I have pursued thee
For this seven years.
Could you have seen me no sooner?"

"Are thou Thought?"
Quote I then,
"Thou couldest wisse me
Where that Do~Well dwells,
And do me that~ to know."

"Do~Well and Do~ Better
And Do~Best, the third,"
Quod he,
"Are three fair virtues
And have not been
Far to find.

U

Sire Do~Well dwells,
   Not a day away
   In a castle,
   That kynde made
   Of four kinds of things.
Of earth and air it is made,
         Melted togethers
With wind and with water,
         Wittily enjoined.

Who so ever is true of his tongue,
And his two hands
 And through his labor,
 Or his lands~
  He wins bread,

And is trusty of tallying,
Takes but his own,
And is not a dingus (drunken?)
Nor dangerous,
Him Do~Well follows.

Do~Better does this right,
And he does much more.
He is low as a lamb
And lovely of speech
And helps all men.

Do~Best is above them both,
And pulls men out of trouble."

I thanked Thought then
  That he, thus, taught me,
    But yet
      I could not savor the sayings,
      And I wanted to learn
      How Do~Well, Do~Better, and Do~Best
Do'en amongst the people.

Thought and I,
Thus,
For three days
We strolled along
Disputing upon Do~Well,
Day after other.

And I awaked therewith
To go forth alone.

The End

And if grace graunte thee
To goo in this wise
Thou shalt se in thy self
Truth sitte in thine herte
In a cheyne of charite
As thou a child were

Click it and clatch it
and set it in thine herte

About the Author

Very little is undoubtedly known about William Langland. His name is uncertain, but Long Will is accepted; his last name might have been either Long Land or one of a few other possibilities. That William lived from 1334(?) until 1394(?) and was born near the area known as the Great Malvern of England is almost certain. During his lifetime William was one of the lucky few who were able to receive an education, and he put it to work. French and Latin were the language of the courts and of well-educated people, but it would be almost 200 years before early days of modern English.

About the Translator

Thomas Edwards only recently returned to returned to college, and is from the midwest. A Fair Field is his first work of this obscure story.

CPSIA information can be obtained
at www.ICGtesting.com
Printed in the USA
LVHW070003231118
598010LV00007B/19/P